tock tick-tock tick-tock tick-tock ti...

tick-tock tick-tock

B. E. Pearson
Elementary School

Donated By: KRYSTAL +KRISTINA RATH

In Honor Of: _____

School Year: _____ 94/95

For John Browne,
John O'Dowdd, and John Williams
E.B.

For Lucy and William
D.P.

Text copyright © 1993 by Eileen Browne
Illustrations copyright © 1993 by David Parkins

First U.S. edition 1994
First published in Great Britain in 1993 by Walker Books Ltd., London.

Library of Congress Cataloging-in-Publication Data is available.

ISBN 1-56402-300-1

10 9 8 7 6 5 4 3 2 1

Printed in Hong Kong

The pictures in this book were done in ink and watercolor.

Candlewick Press
2067 Massachusetts Avenue
Cambridge, Massachusetts 02140

Tick-Tock

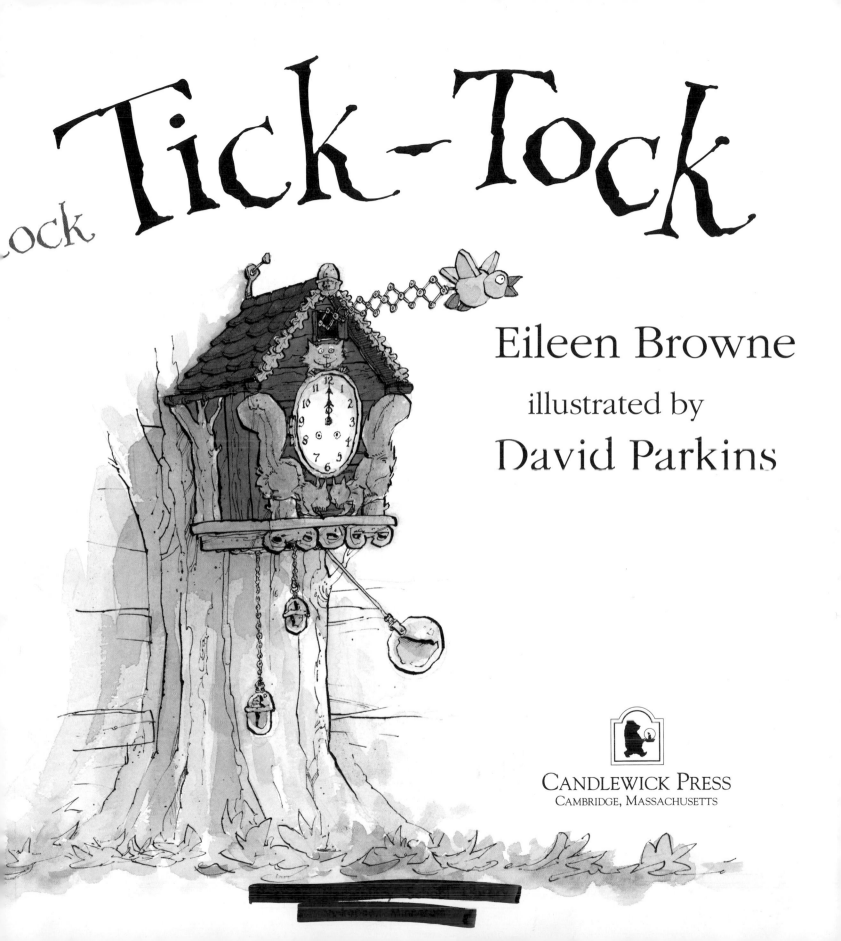

Eileen Browne

illustrated by

David Parkins

CANDLEWICK PRESS
CAMBRIDGE, MASSACHUSETTS

Skip Squirrel and her mom
lived in a tree house
with bouncy squirrel chairs
and a squirrel cuckoo clock.
The clock went,

> *tick-tock . . . tick-tock.*

And the cuckoo popped
out and sang,

> *Cuckoo*

at one o'clock.

> *Cuckoo, cuckoo*

at two o'clock.
And at four o'clock
it sang,

> *Cuckoo*

four times.
"I love that clock,"
said Mom to Skip.

One afternoon Mom had to go out.
Tick-tock . . . tick-tock.
"I'll be back at four," she said.
"And NO JUMPING ON THE CHAIRS!
Something might get broken."
"Okay," said Skip.
They rubbed noses good-bye,
and, with a flick of her tail,
Mom was gone.

"Hi-ya!" Skip's friend,
Brainy, leaped into the tree
house. Skip was so pleased
to see her, she FORGOT
what her mom had said . . .
She JUMPED ON A CHAIR!
So did Brainy.

Boing! Boing!
They bounced
up and down.

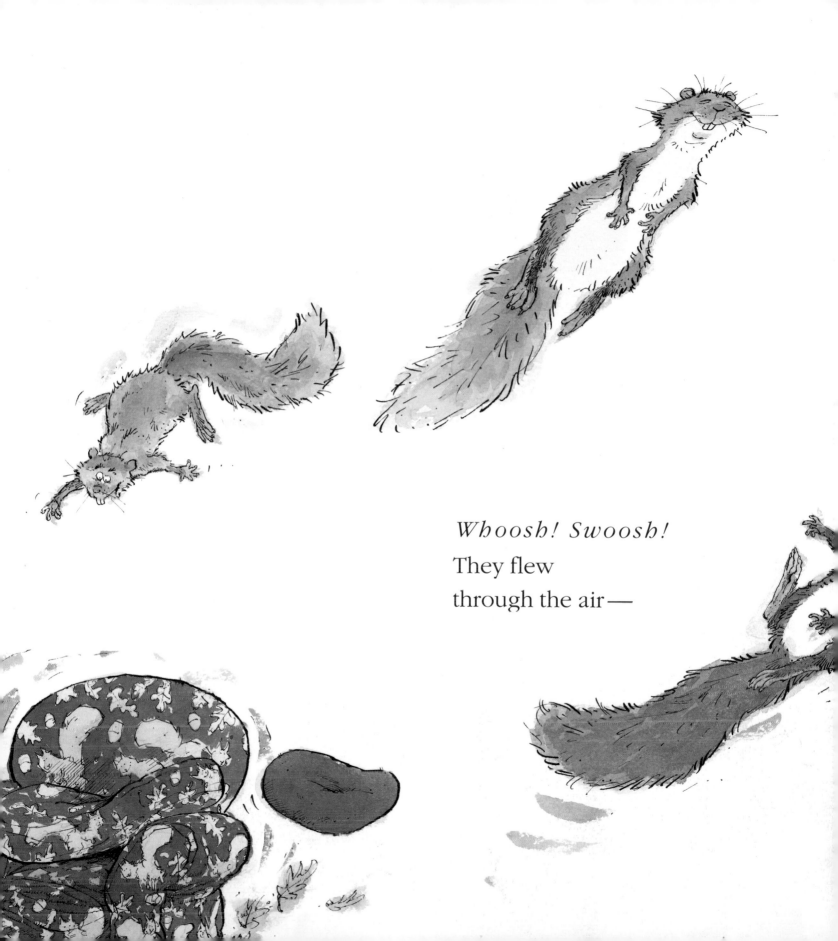

Whoosh! Swoosh!
They flew
through the air—

CRASH!

—into the cuckoo clock.

Tick-tock . . .

tickerty-tockerty . . .

CLUNK!

The cuckoo clock stopped.

"Oh, no!" cried Skip. "It's broken.

Help! Mom will be back at four!"

"Don't panic," said Brainy.

"Relax! We'll take it to Weasel.

She fixes things."

They ran through the woods to Weasel's.

"Can you fix this clock?" asked Skip.
"Let's see," barked Weasel, and opened it up.
"Aha!" she said. "This clock has a puncture!"

Weasel glued on two patches
and pumped in some air.
"Soon have it on the road again,"
she said. "I'll just oil the chain."

Drip . . . drip . . .

Whirr . . . whirr . . .

The clock started!

Tick-tock . . .

tickerty-tockerty . . .

CLUNK!

The cuckoo clock stopped.
"Oh, pedals!" said Weasel. "I can't fix it."
"Oh, NO!" cried Skip. "It's two o'clock.
Mom will be back at four!"
"Calm down," said Brainy. "Never fear!
We'll take it to Hedgehog. She fixes things."

They raced through the fields to Hedgehog's.

"Can you fix this clock?" asked Skip.
"I'll try," snuffled Hedgehog.
She looked underneath.
"Oooh," she said.
"This clock's worn out.
It needs new soles!"

Hedgehog stuck on some soles,
polished the front, and fitted red shoelaces.
"Soon have it back on its feet," she said.
"I'll just hammer this nail in."

Tap . . . tap . . .
Whirr . . . whirr . . .
The clock started!
Tick-tock . . .
tickerty tockerty . . .
CLUNK!

The cuckoo clock stopped.
"Oh, flip-flops!" said Hedgehog. "I can't fix it."
"Oh, NO!" cried Skip. "It's THREE o'clock.
Mom will be back at four!"
"Don't worry," said Brainy. "Keep cool!
We'll take it to Owl. She fixes things."

They rushed through the trees to Owl's.

"Can YOU fix this clock?" asked Skip.
"Of course," said Owl.
"I LOVE fixing clocks.
 Let's have a look."

"What's this?" asked Owl.
"Puncture repairs? Bike oil?
Soles? Shoelaces?"
She pulled off the patches
and cleaned up the oil.
She unstuck the soles
and untied the laces.
Then she tinkered
for ages . . .
and ages . . .
and AGES . . .

Whirr . . . whirr . . .
The cuckoo clock started!
Tick-tock . . . tick-tock . . .
tick-tock . . . tick-tock . . .

"It's working!" cried Skip.
"Yes," said Owl.
"Now, let's hear it
cuckoo!"
"No time," said Skip.
"Thanks, Owl.
But I MUST get this
clock back by four."

Tick-tock . . .
tick-tock . . .
"Don't drop it,"
said Brainy, as they
ran back to Skip's.

Tick-tock . . .
tick-tock . . .
"Don't slip,"
said Skip, as they
climbed up her tree.

Tick-tock . . .
tick-tock . . .
Carefully, they
hung the clock
back on the wall.

It was ONE
MINUTE to four.
"Phew!" said Skip.
She flopped
in a chair.

"See you later!"
said Brainy, and
waved good-bye.

Tick-tock . . . tick-tock . . .
tick-tock . . .
tick-tock . . .
"Hello—o!
I'm home!"
Mom Squirrel
jumped in and
gave Skip a hug.
"Have you been
good?" she asked.

But before Skip
could answer, the
cuckoo popped out
of the clock and
sang . . .

-tock tick-tock tick-tock tick-tock tick-tock tick-tock tick-tock tick-tock tick-